Meg Mackintosh
and
The Mystery in the Locked Library

A Solve-It-Yourself Mystery
by Lucinda Landon

Little, Brown and Company
Boston Toronto London

Books by Lucinda Landon

Meg Mackintosh and the Case of the Missing Babe Ruth Baseball

Meg Mackintosh and the Case of the Curious Whale Watch

Meg Mackintosh and the Mystery at the Medieval Castle

Meg Mackintosh and the Mystery at Camp Creepy

Meg Mackintosh and the Mystery in the Locked Library

First Edition

The characters and events in this book are fictitious. Any similarity to real persons, living or dead, is coincidental and not intended by the author.

Library of Congress Cataloging-in-Publication Data

Landon, Lucinda.
Meg Mackintosh and the mystery in the locked library : a solve-it-yourself mystery / Lucinda Landon.—1st ed.
p. cm.
Summary: Meg investigates the theft of a rare book from a locked library. The reader is challenged to solve the mystery before Meg, using clues in both text and illustrations.
ISBN 0-316-51374-1
[1. Libraries—Fiction. 2. Mystery and detective stories. 3. Literary recreations.] I. Title.
PZ7.L231735Mg 1993
[Fic]—dc20 92-19948

Joy Street Books are published by
Little, Brown and Company (Inc.)

10 9 8 7 6 5 4 3 2 1

BP

Published simultaneously in Canada
by Little, Brown & Company (Canada) Limited

Printed in the United States of America

For Eric Egan

PICNIC ROCK 192
M.M.
Tues.
5:15
George
Meg + Peter
Horace
Plotnik
Wed.
pick up
yogurt
cereal
fruit
popsicles
Meg Mackintosh
HONEY

This cereal looks like bark and twigs," Meg Mackintosh said to her brother Peter.

"I guess Alice thought we'd like it." Peter shrugged. "She bought it just for our visit."

"Hey, look out! You almost ate the coupon." Meg quickly snatched a folded piece of paper from Peter's spoon. "Wait a minute. This doesn't look like a coupon."

"Yeah, it's not shiny enough," said Peter. "Quick! Read it before the ink runs."

Gramps peered over Meg's shoulder. "What is it? A secret message from a cereal factory?"

Meg scanned the note. "It's from Alice!" she said. "Gramps, she's *still* calling you Georgie Porgie."

"She must have snuck the note into the cereal before she went to work at the library," said Gramps. "That's my cousin, sly as ever."

1

DEAR GEORGIE PORGIE, MEG, AND PETER: HELP ME, PLEASE!
GO TO THE LOCKED LIBRARY; THIS ISN'T A TEASE.
I HAD TO HIDE SOMETHING—VERY VALUABLE, I'M SURE.
FOLLOW MY CLUES, FIND IT, AND KEEP IT SECURE.
IT COULD BE STOLEN AFTER THE LIBRARY OPENS AT NOON.
I'VE AN EMERGENCY AT THE DENTIST AND WON'T BE BACK SOON.
CLUE NUMBER ONE IS WHERE TO FIND THE KEY:
IT RHYMES WITH "CROOK STOP" AT THE LIBRARY.
Cousin Alice

"This sounds urgent." Meg reached for her detective knapsack. "A mystery in the locked library — fantastic!"

"Outsmarting thieves!" Peter jumped up. "And I was afraid this would be a boring vacation."

"Life's never boring with Cousin Alice." Gramps sighed. "Now what is she up to, hiding valuable objects? I bet it's just another prank. Remember my missing Babe Ruth baseball?" He shook his head. "Well, you can count me out. I don't want anything to do with her latest scheme."

"But Gramps, you've got to come," Meg pleaded.

"Oh, all right, but only to make sure she doesn't get you in any trouble," said Gramps. "And I'm bringing my radio so I don't miss the ball game."

Meg dug her notebook out of her knapsack and started writing. "Let's brainstorm, Peter. The key is hidden somewhere that rhymes with *crook stop.*"

"Took mop?" Peter suggested. "Come on. We'll figure it out when we get there." They headed for the door.

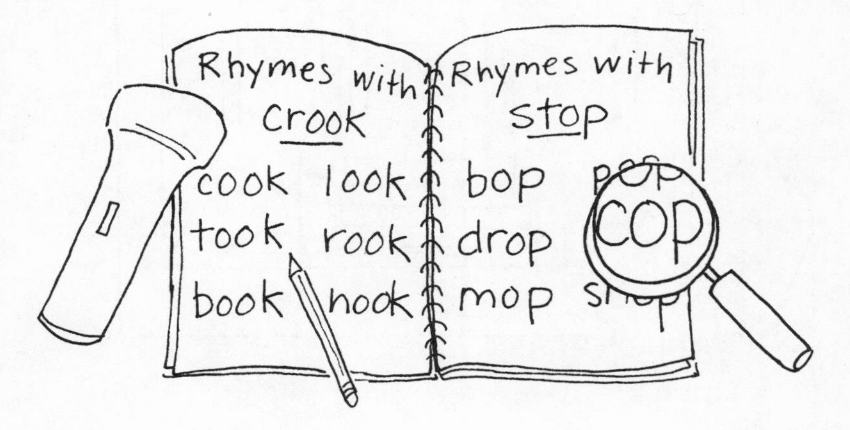

WHERE DO *YOU* THINK THE KEY COULD BE?

The library was only a few blocks' walk from Alice's house.

"What exactly do you think we're supposed to look for?" Peter asked.

"It must be pretty important," said Meg. She took out her instant camera and viewed the scene.

"You know Alice," said Gramps. "She loves clues and mysteries. And she's not going to make it easy for you." Meg focused her camera on the library and snapped a picture. Then she noticed something.

"Hey, I know where the key is!" Meg exclaimed. "At the *book drop!* That rhymes with *crook stop.*"

"That's so obvious." Peter rolled his eyes.

"Then why didn't *you* get it?" They raced up the steps and began searching the book drop for the key.

"If it's dropped inside, we'll have to do the old chewing-gum-and-string trick to get it," Peter said. "Feel around underneath. Maybe the key is taped to the bottom."

"You're right!" Meg called out. "Here it is. It's got a note with it, too."

2
HERE'S CLUE TWO: NOW WATCH THE CLOCK,
AND CHECK OUT AN OLD SHERLOCK.
BE SURE TO GO TO THE RIGHT SECTION.
CHECKING DATES IS GOOD DETECTION.
P.S. PLEASE LOCK THE DOOR BEHIND YOU.

WHERE SHOULD MEG GO NEXT?

They quietly entered the cool, dim library. Peter flicked on the lights while Meg relocked the door.

"Sherlock? Alice *must* mean Sherlock Holmes, the world's greatest detective," said Meg.

" 'Watch the clock,' " Peter added. "Maybe something's hidden in that old clock."

"Maybe," Meg replied. "But I think Alice means we have to keep track of the time . . . and hurry."

"Now why would Alice want you to hurry?" Gramps

asked. "There's no one else around."

"She's afraid someone might steal the valuable object after the library opens at noon," Meg replied.

"I wish I had my camera," said Peter. "Meg-O, let me borrow yours. Maybe I'll spot something valuable."

"Okay." Meg handed it over. "But don't drop it."

Just then, they heard a sound from behind a shelf of books.

An older boy stepped out from behind the encyclopedias. "Hey, what's going on here?" he asked.

"I'm Alice Mackintosh's cousin," Gramps explained.

"She gave us a key," added Meg.

"We're solving a mystery," Peter blurted out.

"Shhh, big mouth." Meg elbowed Peter.

The boy looked puzzled. "Well, Alice is the head librarian. If it's okay with her, it's okay with me." He shook hands with Gramps. "I'm Gerry. I help out around here."

A ringing phone interrupted them, and Gerry went to the checkout desk to answer it.

"That was Alice's dentist," he told them after he hung up. "She hasn't shown up for her appointment."

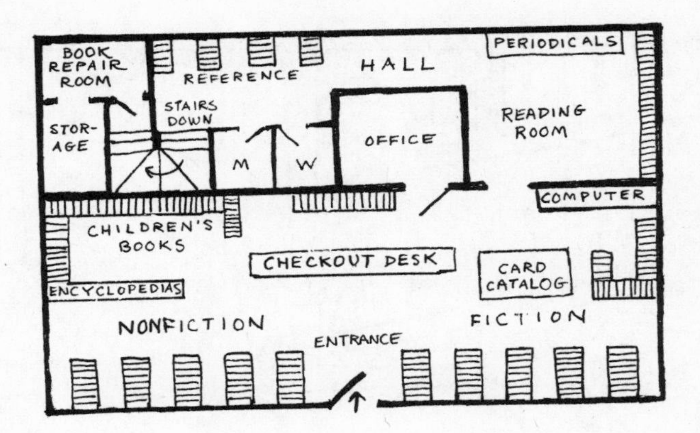

"Oh, she's always late," said Gramps as he looked at the map of the library posted on the wall. "I'll be in the reading room listening to the game. Let me know if you need me."

"Come on, Peter." Meg tugged his sleeve. "Let's get to work."

Peter was busy taking photos. "Okay, where do we start?"

WHERE WOULD YOU START TO LOOK?

"The clue says, 'Check out an old Sherlock.' Maybe there's a clue over there." Meg headed to the checkout desk. She began flipping through the file cards on books that were checked out. "No Sherlock Holmes books here," she called over to Peter.

Peter was frantically pulling out card catalog drawers. "It's already ten-thirty, and the library opens at noon. That doesn't give us much time. Alice must have had a hunch the valuable object was in danger."

Meg tapped the desktop impatiently, then reread the clue. " 'Be sure to go to the right section. Checking dates is good detection.' "

"I can't find anything under *Sherlock*," Peter muttered. "Come on, let's take a look in the biography section under *H*."

"Better think again, Peter," said Meg.

WHAT WAS PETER'S MISTAKE?

"We should look in the *fiction* section, not in biographies," Meg told him. "Sherlock Holmes is a fictitious character, written from the imagination."

"Oh, right," said Peter. "We should look under the *author's* last name."

"Exactly," said Meg. "And the author is Sir Arthur Conan Doyle, so we should look in fiction under *D*, for Doyle. Let's go!"

"You *would* know that," said Peter.

They raced to the fiction bookshelves.

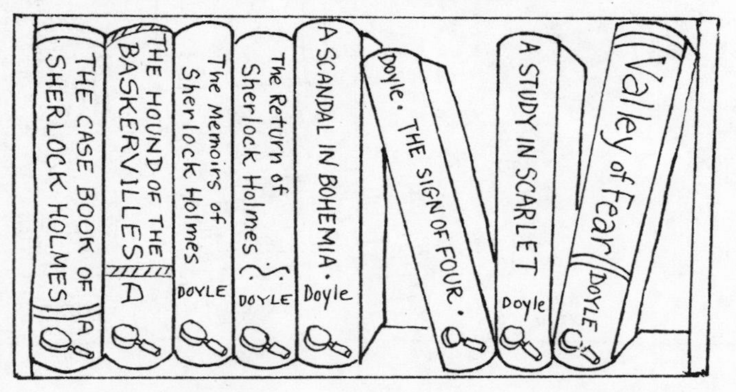

Meg ran her fingers along the backs of the old books. "Alice sure is a mystery fan. See how she puts little magnifying glass stickers on the spines of all the mystery books?"

"Yeah, and look at all the Sherlock Holmes books!" exclaimed Peter as they began opening the books and searching for clues. "What do these books have to do with the valuable object?"

"I don't know yet," said Meg. She checked her watch. "But we have to find out, and soon."

Ten minutes later, they were both discouraged.

"Nothing," said Peter.

"Me either. Not a scrap of paper. Remember, Alice can be pretty tricky in the clue department. She wouldn't have written a message *inside* a book, would she?"

"Librarians *never* write in books," Peter said. Then he reread the clue. "Except . . ."

"Except what?" asked Meg.

WHAT IS PETER GETTING AT?

"The clue says, 'Checking dates is good detection,' " said Peter. "You thought Alice meant checking the file for books that are due back at the library, but maybe she means checking the due date at the *back* of the book. Some libraries are computerized, but it looks like Alice still stamps the due dates by hand. That's the only place where she would *dare* write in a book."

"Good thinking," said Meg. She examined the date card of each book.

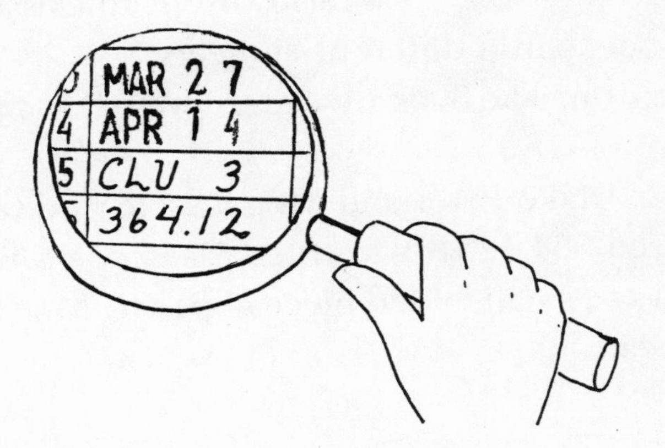

"Look at this Sherlock Holmes book, *The Hound of the Baskervilles,*" Meg pointed out. "Instead of a date stamped, there's a number penciled in."

"It can't mean March 64, 1912," said Peter.

"Definitely not." Meg ripped a corner of paper out of her notebook and jotted down the number.

WHAT COULD THE NUMBER MEAN?

"This looks like a number from the Dewey decimal system," said Meg. "Libraries use it to classify nonfiction books into different subjects."

"Come on. The 300s are over there." Peter jumped up.

It didn't take Peter and Meg long to find the book numbered 364.12. It was titled *Detective Skills*, and inside was a small folded piece of paper. Meg opened it and read:

"Deerstalker? Isn't that the kind of hat Sherlock Holmes wears?" asked Peter.

"Only in the movies, not in the books," Meg said. "Alice might mean for us to use our thinking caps." She flipped open her notebook to decode the message.

Suddenly there was a noise at the door.

"*Ssshhhhh!* What's that?" said Peter.

The lock in the front door clicked, and a young woman stepped in. "Hello? What's going on?" she asked Peter and Meg. "The library isn't open yet."

"It's okay, Caroline." Gerry poked his head out from behind a nearby bookshelf. "These are Alice's cousins. She gave them a key."

"Our grandfather is in the reading room," Meg explained.

"Probably snoring," Peter added.

Caroline looked confused. "Alice mentioned you were coming to visit, but I forgot. Well, it's nice to meet you," she said. "What are you up to today, Gerry?"

"Just the usual cleaning up. Did you see the box of old books your uncle donated to the library yesterday?"

"Oh, I've hardly had a chance. I wonder if Alice started cataloging them." She turned lightly on her heels and walked straight to the office.

"Yoo-hoo! Ms. Mackintosh?" A voice from behind made them jump.

"You shouldn't sneak up on people like that!" Peter protested.

"So sorry," the bearded man apologized. "I didn't want to interrupt. This is a public library, isn't it?"

"Yes, but it's not open yet." Caroline had stepped out of the office. "I'm Caroline Stone, librarian's assistant. I must have forgotten to relock the door."

"I'll lock it," Gerry volunteered.

"I'm Horace Plotnik," the man said. He fumbled for a minute, then pulled a crumpled business card out of his pocket. "I'm an authority on antiques. Ms. Alice Mackintosh called me to appraise a valuable object."

"Oh, I see," said Caroline.

"Well, she's not in yet," said Gerry. "She's at the dentist."

"Then if you don't mind, I'll wait." Mr. Plotnik glanced at the old clock. "I am a bit early, but I must say I'm curious to see what she's got." As he headed to the reading room, he peered at Meg's notes. "I love word puzzles! May I help?"

"No, thanks," said Meg. She covered her notes.

"Did you hear that?" Peter whispered to Meg. "Whatever it is we're looking for must be worth a lot!"

"And we'd better hurry up and find it before anyone else drops by," Meg muttered.

When Gerry stepped up to check out his own books, Meg quietly covered her notes again. "You're a mystery fan, too!" she said, noticing the titles.

"Love them," said Gerry. "Alice always tells me when a new one comes in."

"Have you worked here long?" Peter asked him.

"A few months. I'm saving up for some powerful binoculars."

"For spying?" Meg guessed.

"Nah . . . for baseball games." Gerry laughed.

Caroline turned to Meg and Peter. "What are you two working on?"

"Looks like they're trying to solve some kind of secret code." Gerry peered over Meg's shoulder. "I think it's something to do with Sherlock Holmes. Just kid stuff."

"This isn't kid stuff!" protested Peter.

"Sherlock Holmes? He's one of my favorite detectives." Caroline smiled. "Don't let me interrupt your fun, but if I were you, I'd look down in the book repair room. There's a very good book about codes down there being rebinded."

Meg closed her notebook, slid off her seat, and headed for the stairs. "I've almost cracked the code, but let's check it out anyway," she whispered to Peter.

"I bet Gerry follows — he's been spying on us," Peter whispered back.

"Gerald, don't forget to take out the recycling bin," Caroline reminded him. "The truck will be here soon."

"Whoops!" Gerry smacked his forehead. "I'll get it — right after I show them the way downstairs." He dashed after Meg and Peter.

From the stairs to the cellar, Meg heard a pounding on the book repair room door. It was bolted from the outside. "Hey!" she cried. "What's that noise?"

"*Hurry up!*" Peter called out to Gerry.

"Don't worry — I have a key!" Gerry hurried down the stairs. Gramps and Mr. Plotnik had heard the commotion and came following behind them.

Gerry fumbled for the right key on his key ring, then finally sprung the door open.

It was Alice!

"Alice!!! Are you all right?" they all exclaimed.

"Thank goodness!" cried Alice. "I got locked in here hours ago! Who's been blaring the radio with the baseball game? George, it had to be you. What are you doing with a radio on in the library?" She caught her breath. "Oh, my aching tooth!"

"Sorry, Alice," said Gramps. "Are you all right? What happened?"

"Oh, I'm all right, except for this toothache. I was on my way to the dentist, but I came here first because I'd forgotten the book I was repairing for Dr. Hugo. A breeze must have blown the door shut, and then the lock jammed." Alice held her jaw. "I've been banging on the door, but you couldn't hear me because of that noisy radio!"

Meanwhile, Peter examined the lock. "But Alice, this lock couldn't possibly catch all by itself. Someone must have shut you in there on purpose!"

"That's ridiculous! You've been reading too many mysteries," said Alice. "Now let's talk upstairs."

Meg whispered to Peter, "Do you really think someone locked her in?"

"Looks that way to me," said Peter. "I smell a rat."

Just then, Alice noticed Mr. Plotnik behind Gramps. "Oh, hello," she said. "You're a bit early for our appointment. I'll be with you in a few minutes."

"No hurry, ma'am." Mr. Plotnik looked up from his antique guidebook. "I've got plenty of time."

As Alice herded Meg and Peter toward the stairs, she asked, "Did you find *it?*"

"Not yet, Alice. We've *almost* got it," Meg answered, and then she practically flew up the stairs. Quickly fetching her notebook from the checkout desk, Meg finished decoding the message and joined Peter and Alice in the reading room.

HAVE YOU CRACKED THE CODE YET?

Directly over the chair where Gramps had been sitting all morning was a sign: QUIET, PLEASE. Meg reached up behind it, and sure enough, there was another clue. It was wadded up in a ball.

Gerry snuck up behind her. "Did you find something?" he asked. "Where was the clue?"

"Behind the 'Quiet, Please,' " Meg said.

"Behind the what?" Gerry asked.

" 'Quiet, Please!' " repeated Peter.

"Don't tell me to be quiet," shouted Gerry.

"I didn't!" Peter hollered back.

"What's going on?" Mr. Plotnik hustled into the reading room, followed by Gramps.

"*Sshhh! Quiet, please, everybody!*" Caroline had come away from the computer desk. "Alice, are you all right? Gerry just told me what happened!"

"I'm okay, Caroline." Alice clicked off Gramps's radio. "Go ahead and read the clue, Meg. Then I'll explain everything."

Meg smoothed out the wadded piece of paper and read:

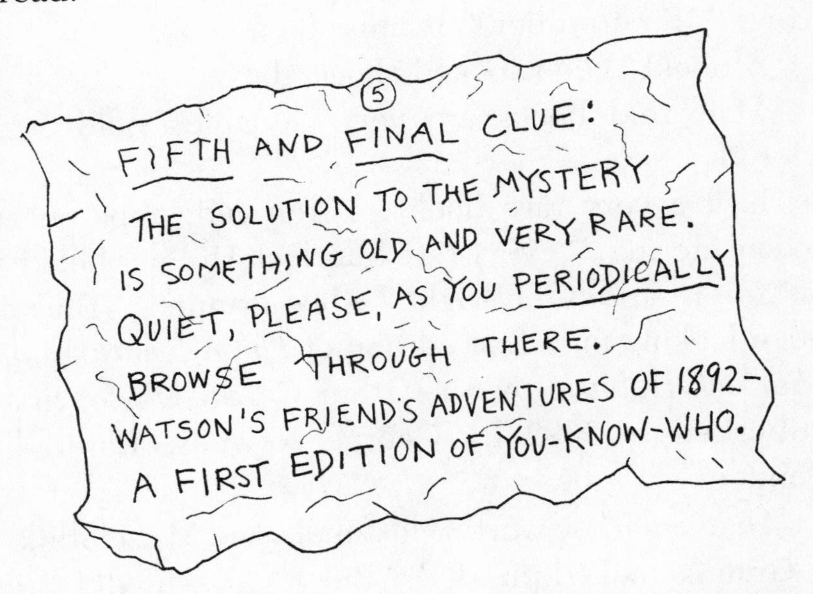

5
FIFTH AND FINAL CLUE:
THE SOLUTION TO THE MYSTERY
IS SOMETHING OLD AND VERY RARE.
QUIET, PLEASE, AS YOU PERIODICALLY
BROWSE THROUGH THERE.
WATSON'S FRIEND'S ADVENTURES OF 1892–
A FIRST EDITION OF YOU-KNOW-WHO.

"Hmmm. 'Watson's friend.' I think I know what we're looking for," said Meg. "And I think I know where it is, too."

WHAT ARE THEY LOOKING FOR?
WHERE DO YOU THINK IT IS?

"Dr. John Watson was friend and assistant detective to none other than Sherlock Holmes," declared Meg. " 'First edition?' It must be a book!"

"A book!" Peter looked shocked.

"Many old books are very valuable," said Mr. Plotnik.

"Is it a very rare book?" Peter said, apparently reconsidering. "A very rare Sherlock Holmes book?"

"You're absolutely right!" Alice grinned. "You've been looking for a first edition of *The Adventures of Sherlock Holmes,* by Sir Arthur Conan Doyle, first published in 1892 by George Newnes, Limited, London."

"That *would* be worth a fortune!" said Mr. Plotnik.

Gramps looked puzzled. "But Alice, why did you hide it? Why didn't you bring it home if you were so worried?"

"It's library policy not to remove valuable objects," Alice explained. "The collection of old books just came yesterday. I was worried that something might happen to the Sherlock Holmes book before I could get it appraised and get a proper bookcase to lock it in, so I hid it for safekeeping. Then I planted the clues so you would find it and keep it safe until I returned from the dentist. I was afraid I might be there for hours, and then who knows what could have happened to it!"

"And you were also testing our library skills," added Peter.

"Oh, I am a bit of a schemer," Alice admitted. "Now reread the clue, and you'll find the book."

Peter glanced at the note. "*Periodically* is underlined. It might have to do with periodicals."

"Right — that's library talk for magazines," said Meg.

Meg and Peter looked through the shelf of magazines beside the "Quiet, Please" sign, but they came up empty-handed.

"Well, Alice, here's a mystery for you," said Peter. "I detect your *Sherlock* is missing!"

"*What?*" Alice cried. She jumped up and shuffled through the magazines.

WHAT DO YOU THINK HAPPENED?

"Oh, no! Someone *did* steal the book!" cried Alice. "I'm sure it was here this morning when I came in. Peter, maybe you were right — maybe someone did lock me in!"

While everyone else continued to search the shelves for the missing book, Meg motioned Peter over to the checkout desk. "Alice couldn't be mistaken about where she hid the book — she was so exact about it. It must have been stolen!"

"We've got to find it," added Peter. "We're the ones who were supposed to find it and keep it safe."

"Let's see those instant photos you took this morning," suggested Meg. "Maybe we can learn something from them."

Peter fished the photos out of his pocket. But when he tried to clear a space on the checkout desk to view them, he accidentally knocked over Gerry's pile of

books, sending pencils, mail, and everything else flying.

"Careful for Louisa May Alcott!" Meg nimbly caught the statue. As she helped straighten things, she noticed something strange. "Hmm," she said. "This is weird."

"This mystery sure *is* weird," Peter replied. "I bet someone broke into the library early this morning."

"But Alice saw the book when she came in, remember?" Meg shook her head. "Anyway, how would the thief know where the book was hidden?"

"Hey, Meg-O, let me borrow your magnifying glass," said Peter. "I see something in one of these photos that might prove when the book was stolen."

DO YOU SEE ANYTHING THAT MIGHT HELP PROVE WHEN THE BOOK WAS STOLEN?

"Look!" exclaimed Peter. "In this photograph, you can see the corner of *The Adventures of Sherlock Holmes* between two magazines!" Gramps was sitting right next to it all morning. It would have been impossible for someone to have taken it without his noticing."

"Excellent, Peter!" said Meg. "But the photo shows that the book must have been stolen while we were here." She frowned. "Hey — Gramps did leave the reading room once. He and Mr. Plotnik came downstairs when we found Alice."

"I'll go check the door and windows and see if it looks as if someone broke in," said Peter. "You brainstorm."

As Meg jotted in her notebook, she listened to the others talking in the reading room.

"Alice, are you sure it's missing? You didn't accidentally misplace it?" asked Gramps.

"I'm positive!" Alice insisted.

"You mean I came all the way over here for nothing?" Mr. Plotnik sounded annoyed. "Maybe those kids hid it as a trick!"

"There must be some reasonable explanation," said Caroline. "Gerry, did you see it?"

"Don't look at me!" Gerry mumbled. "I didn't take it!"

"Just finish your chores," Caroline said softly. "And please take the recycling bin out to the curb and the mail to the mailbox."

"Well, I have other appointments." Mr. Plotnik stood up, tried to smooth down his jacket, and picked up his briefcase.

"I think you'd better stay here until we get this settled," Gramps told him politely. "Alice, we should call the police if you think someone broke into the library."

"Oooww, now I'm really in pain," moaned Alice. "Thieves and toothaches in one day. This is horrid!"

Gramps put his hand on her shoulder. "Don't worry — we'll figure this out."

Meg twisted one pigtail and thought hard about what could have happened to the valuable book.

WHAT DO YOU THINK HAPPENED?
WHO ARE THE SUSPECTS?

A few minutes later, Peter returned to the desk. "I checked all the doors and windows in the library. They are definitely locked. No one could have broken in." He leaned over Meg's shoulder and read her notes with wide eyes.

Mr. Plotnik
He collects rare objects and came early for his appointment with Alice. Now he wants to leave. He loves puzzles
ANTIQUES PRICE GUIDE
Gerry
He has his own key to the library. He's been snooping around. He loves mysteries. He's saving $ for an expensive item.
Caroline Stone
She has her own key to the library. Her uncle gave some books to the library.
Gramps
Maybe he wants to get back at Alice for all of her pranks!
nah!

"That proves it," said Meg firmly. "The Sherlock Holmes book had to be taken by Mr. Plotnik, Caroline, or Gerry. Hmm. Gerry did check out an armful of mysteries," she continued. "Maybe he's a mystery book collector. But if Gerry took the Sherlock Holmes book this morning, why would he hang around so long?"

"To let Alice out!" said Peter. "He felt guilty. Or else because he couldn't find the book at first. How could anyone find it without messing up the whole library? No one knew where Alice had hid it."

Meg thought for a second. "You've got a point there, Peter. When Gerry saw us trying to solve a mystery about Sherlock Holmes, he hoped we'd lead him to it."

"Now he's waiting for the opportunity to get it out of the library. I'll look around and see if I can find where he hid it. If we can catch him with it red-handed, we'll really crack the case."

"But how could anyone find the book before us?" Meg wondered. She dug Alice's clues out of her knapsack, hoping they would jar her memory. She was determined to figure this out.

"Hmmm. That's strange," she said to herself.

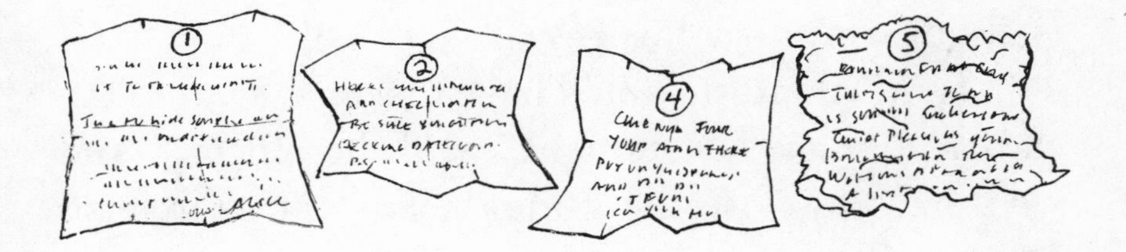

DO YOU NOTICE ANYTHING STRANGE
ABOUT THE CLUES?

"Peter, look," Meg said. "The fifth clue was all crumpled when we found it, but the others were folded neatly. *Maybe* someone read it *before* us."

"Possible. But who had the opportunity?" asked Peter.

Suddenly there was a knock at the front door, and Peter ran to open it. It was a policewoman.

Alice tried to explain what had happened.

"Let me get this straight." The officer sounded puzzled. "This valuable book was hidden on purpose, but then it was stolen? What exactly is it worth?"

"Many thousands of dollars," said Alice. "Especially to a mystery lover."

"Ms. Mackintosh, you'll have to come down to the station to make a statement," said the officer. "And we'll have to close the library so we can search for clues and the book."

"Close the library!" Alice cried. "This is a disaster!"

"Come on, Alice," said Gramps. "Why don't you

call your dentist? Then at least your tooth will feel better."

"I just did. Dr. Hugo's calling me back." Alice sighed. "Okay, everybody, I'm locking up the library."

Meg and Peter gathered up their detecting things. Caroline went to get her pocketbook. Gramps got his radio. Mr. Plotnik picked up his briefcase.

"Where's Gerry?" asked Alice.

"Here I am," Gerry said as he bounded into the room. I finally remembered to put the recycling bin out — just in time."

"We've got to tell them about Gerry," Peter whispered to Meg. "Quick, before he gets away with it!"

"Just give me a second." Meg studied her notes.

"But your notes *are* wrong about one thing," Peter pointed out.

"What?" said Meg. She stared at her notebook.

WHAT'S WRONG IN MEG'S NOTES?

"Not *everyone* went downstairs to rescue Alice," said Peter.

"Hey — you're right." Meg chewed her pencil.

"Come on, Meg, Peter," Alice interrupted them. "Caroline, would you please turn off the computer and the lights? And Gerry, would you please mail these letters?"

Suddenly Meg was reminded of something on the desk, and all the pieces of the puzzle fell into place. "Wait!" she called out. "I think I know what happened to the Sherlock Holmes book!"

Mr. Plotnik looked at Meg. "Who are you? Sherlock Holmes's great-granddaughter?"

"Meg *is* a good detective," said Gramps. "What have you deduced, Meg?"

Meg began to explain: "The only way to find the Sherlock Holmes book was to read the last clue, the one behind the "Quiet, Please" sign, which said exactly where it was hidden. That means someone deciphered *Quiet, Please* in the code before I did. Only one person had a chance to do that."

"Who?" they all asked.

WHO HAD THE OPPORTUNITY?

"Caroline," said Meg.

"Caroline?" All heads turned in disbelief.

"I was almost finished decoding the clue in my notebook when Caroline suggested we look downstairs in the book repair room for a book about codes. That's when we found Alice. Gramps and Mr. Plotnik heard us and came right downstairs, too. But Caroline stayed upstairs, where I had left my notebook — on the checkout desk. That's when she had the opportunity to peek in my notebook, quickly finish deciphering the code, and take *The Adventures of Sherlock Holmes* before we came back upstairs." Meg paused for a second. "And I have a feeling she knew Alice was downstairs, because *she* locked her in."

"This is absurd!" Caroline said sharply. "What are you talking about!"

"There's more proof," said Meg. "You left a careless clue. After you read the last clue, you were in such a hurry that you crumpled it up and stuffed it behind the "Quiet, Please" sign. So the last clue isn't folded neatly like the others."

"Meg's right," Alice blurted out. "I did fold all the clues."

"Is this some kind of a joke?" Caroline's voice shook with anger. "I work here!"

"That's right. So you have a key to get into the library anytime," Meg continued. "*And* you have a motive. I heard Gerry say that your uncle had donated the box of old books. I bet you knew that book was valuable and thought your uncle should have given it to you."

"You're all wrong. I'm sure the book has only been misplaced," Caroline insisted. "It might have been accidentally thrown out with the old newspapers I asked Gerry to put in the recycling bin today. This is all a big misunderstanding!"

"The recycling bin!" yelled Gerry. "*Oh, no!* I think I heard the crew pick it up already!"

"Uh-oh, Meg." Peter looked worried. "Maybe you made a mistake. I thought the book might be in the recycling bin!"

"It's okay, Gerry," said Meg. "I think I know where *The Adventures of Sherlock Holmes* really is."

WHERE IS THE BOOK?

"Gerry has it," said Meg.

"I knew he had something to do with it," said Peter.

"No, he didn't." Meg shook her head. "It's in the package Gerry's about to mail. Caroline put that package on the desk *after* we came upstairs. I'm sure it wasn't there before. When Peter accidentally knocked over the pile of books and mail, I noticed a new large package, which Caroline had addressed to herself. I thought that was suspicious. I just *now* figured out that it was a quick way to get the book out of the library — have Gerry mail it."

"Mailing a package to yourself, Caroline?" asked Alice. "That seems a bit odd. Surely you wouldn't mind opening the package, just to prove it one way or the other."

"No, you open it." Caroline turned away.

Gerry handed the package to Alice. She ripped it open, and sure enough, the old Sherlock Holmes book was inside.

"Caroline! How could you?" exclaimed Alice.

"That book is worth a fortune!" Caroline cried. "And it could have been mine. Uncle Jack should have given me those old books! I thought I could sneak one out of the box without anyone noticing. I came in early this morning. I didn't think Alice would be here. When I heard her downstairs, I panicked. I didn't want her to see me snooping around. So I shut the door on her. But I still couldn't find the book! Then I heard Gerry coming, so I left.

"I did come back to let you out," Caroline explained to Alice, "but everyone was here. When I learned the kids were solving a Sherlock Holmes mystery, I realized that you must have hidden the book and that I had a chance to find it before them. I never thought it would come to this."

Alice shook her head. "I'm sorry, Caroline. But I think I'll have to look for a new assistant."

Meanwhile, Mr. Plotnik had been examining the book. "This meets all the specifications of an authentic first edition of *The Adventures of Sherlock Holmes*," he said.

"It is a real treasure," Gramps told Alice. "I know the library will be a good home for it . . . once you get a safe library case."

"Nice detecting, Meg and Peter," Alice said. "This turned out to be quite a mystery!"

"Alice," Gerry called out. "Telephone."

"I detect it's your dentist," said Meg.

"He can take you this afternoon," added Peter.

"Thank goodness," said Alice, "but how do you know?"

"It's elementary, my dear." Gramps grinned.

"We are detectives," Meg said, laughing.

"And very clever ones." Alice hugged them. "Very clever indeed!"

100th Anniversary Celebration
1892-1992
CITY OF LONDON
The
Adventures
of
Sherlock Holmes
by
A. Conan Doyle

CASE CLOSED.

Libraries